cloverleaf books™

Our American Symbols

What Is Inside the Lincoln Memorial?

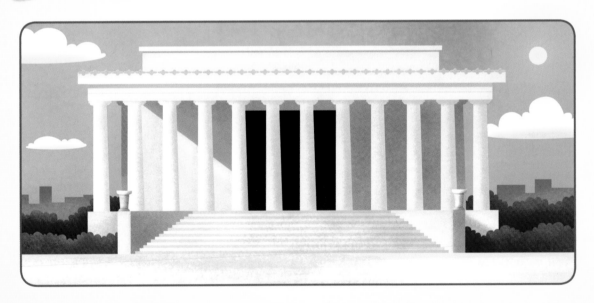

Martha E. H. Rustad

illustrated by Kyle Poling

M MILLBROOK PRESS · MINNEAPOLIS

For Jerry and Dawn —M.E.H.R.

For Dad and Mom, Joanne and Herman,
Donna and Ned, and Eva Jean and Jim
                                    —K.P.

Millbrook Press
A division of Lerner Publishing Group, Inc.
241 First Avenue North
Minneapolis, MN 55401 USA

For reading levels and more information, look up this title at
www.lernerbooks.com.

Images in this book used with the permission of: © Arthit
Kaeoratanapattama/Shutterstock.com, p. 23.

Main body text set in Slappy Inline 18/28.
Typeface provided by T26.

Library of Congress Cataloging-in-Publication Data

Rustad, Martha E. H. (Martha Elizabeth Hillman), 1975–
    What Is Inside the Lincoln Memorial / by Martha E. H. Rustad; illustrated
  by Kyle Poling.
        pages   cm. — (Cloverleaf books: American symbols)
    Includes index.
    ISBN: 978-1-4677-2135-6 (lib. bdg. : alk. paper)
    ISBN: 978-1-4677-4772-1 (eBook)
    1. Lincoln Memorial (Washington, D.C.)—Juvenile literature. 2. Lincoln,
  Abraham, 1809-1865—Monuments—Washington (D.C.)—Juvenile literature.
  3. Washington (D.C.)—Buildings, structures, etc.—Juvenile literature. I.
  Poling, Kyle, illustrator. II. Title.
  F203.4.L73R87 2015
  975.3—dc23   2013037338

Manufactured in the United States of America
1 – BP – 7/15/14

TABLE OF CONTENTS

Chapter One
**A Visit to the
Lincoln Memorial.....4**

Chapter Two
Inside the Memorial.....12

Chapter Three
Remembering Lincoln.....18

Make a Hand Impression....22

Glossary....23

To Learn More....24

Index....24

A Visit to the Lincoln Memorial

Our class is going on a **field trip!**
Mr. Williams makes us guess where.

"It has to do with the person on this **penny**," he hints.

"George Washington?" guesses Greg.

"Abe Lincoln?" says Timothy.

"That's right! It's **Abraham Lincoln**," our teacher says. "He was the sixteenth **president** of the United States."

"Do you know what building is on the back of this penny?" asks Mr. Williams.

"Is it the White House?" Sandy asks.
"No, it is the **Lincoln Memorial**," says Mr. Williams.

"What's a memorial?" asks Elizabeth.
"It's a **building** or **statue** that helps us
remember someone who died," answers our teacher.
We look out the bus windows. There it is!

Ranger May meets us outside the memorial. She is our **tour guide**.

"Many parts of this building tell us something about Abraham Lincoln. Can you count the **columns?**" she asks.

Abraham Lincoln
was president from
1861 to 1865.

"One . . . two . . . three . . . twelve!" says Maria.
"More columns help hold up the back and sides
too. In all, there are **thirty-six**," Ranger May
tells us. "That's because there were thirty-six
US states at the end of the time when Lincoln
was president."

9

"Abraham Lincoln was president during the **Civil War**," says Ranger May. "This war began when the Southern states formed their own country in **1861**." "Why did they do that?" asks Chloe.

Northern States

Southern States

"Some white people in the South kept black people as slaves," Ranger May tells us. "But President Lincoln thought **slavery** was **wrong**. Southerners worried that he would end slavery. So they broke away. Lincoln fought the Civil War to keep all the states together."

"What happened to the slaves?" asks Asher.

"Lincoln helped **end slavery** in **1865**. The Civil War ended that year too," Ranger May says.

Slaves were owned by other people. Many slaves worked on big farms. They had to do what their masters told them to do. They were not paid for their work. They were not free.

Chapter Two
Inside the Memorial

We climb the steps.
We look up at the **statue**
of President Lincoln.
He is sitting in a chair.

The statue of Abraham Lincoln is 19 feet (5.8 meters) tall. If Abe could stand up, he would be 28 feet (8.5 m) tall. That's about as tall as five adults!

We learn that a man named **Daniel Chester French** designed the statue. It is carved from twenty-eight blocks of **marble!** Workers put them together like a puzzle when the building was ready.

"What are all those words on the walls?" asks Eric.

"They are from two speeches by President Lincoln," says Ranger May. "In one, he said that our country's founders wanted **everyone** to be **free**. In the other, he said that all the states should come back **together** as one country."

FOUR SCORE AND SEVEN YEARS AGO OUR FATHERS BROUGHT FORTH ON THIS CONTINENT A NEW NATION CONCEIVED IN LIBERTY AND DEDICA~ TED TO THE PROPOSITION THAT ALL MEN ARE CREATED EQUAL
NOW WE ARE ENGAGED IN A GREAT CIVIL WAR TESTING WHETHER THAT NATION OR ANY NATION SO CON~ CEIVED AND SO DEDICATED CAN LONG ENDURE . WE ARE MET ON A GREAT BATTLEFIELD OF THAT WAR . WE HAVE COME TO DEDICATE A PORTION OF THAT FIELD AS A FINAL RESTING PLACE FOR THOSE WHO HERE GAVE THEIR LIVES THAT THAT NATION MIGHT LIVE . IT IS ALTOGETHER FIT~ TING AND PROPER THAT WE SHOULD DO THIS . BUT IN A LARGER SENSE WE CAN NOT DEDICATE~WE CAN NOT CONSECRATE~WE CAN NOT HALLOW~ THIS GROUND . THE BRAVE MEN LIV~ ING AND DEAD WHO STRUGGLED HERE HAVE CONSECRATED IT FAR ABOVE OUR POOR POWER TO ADD OR DETRACT THE WORLD WILL LITTLE NOTE NOR LONG REMEMBER WHAT WE SAY HERE BUT IT CAN NEVER FORGET WHAT THEY DID HERE . IT IS FOR US THE LIVING RATHER TO BE DEDICATED HERE TO THE UNFINISHED WORK WHICH THEY WHO FOUGHT HERE HAVE THUS FAR SO NOBLY ADVANCED . IT IS RATHER FOR US TO BE HERE DEDICATED TO THE GREAT TASK REMAINING BEFORE US~ THAT FROM THESE HONORED DEAD WE TAKE INCREASED DEVOTION TO THAT CAUSE FOR WHICH THEY GAVE THE LAST FULL MEASURE OF DEVOTION~ THAT WE HERE HIGHLY RESOLVE THAT THESE DEAD SHALL NOT HAVE DIED IN VAIN~THAT THIS NATION UNDER GOD SHALL HAVE A NEW BIRTH OF FREEDOM~ AND THAT GOVERNMENT OF THE PEOPLE BY THE PEOPLE FOR THE PEOPLE SHALL NOT PERISH FROM THE EARTH .

Ranger May points out the paintings above the speeches.

"I see an angel!" says Tabitha.

"The angel is freeing the slaves from their chains," explains Ranger May. "We remember President Lincoln for working to end slavery."

A painting done on a wall is called a mural. The murals in the Lincoln Memorial were made by Jules Guerin. He also made murals in buildings in other US cities.

"Did the president die in the war?" asks Greg.

"No," says Mr. Williams. "But he was killed at a play just five days after the war ended. A man named **John Wilkes Booth** shot him. Booth thought Lincoln's ideas for the country were wrong."

Planning for the Lincoln Memorial started in 1867. Construction didn't begin until 1914. It was finished in 1922.

"Did they bury Lincoln here?" asks Violet.

"No," explains Ranger May. "Abraham Lincoln is buried in Springfield, Illinois. That's where he lived for many years. The memorial was built later."

Chapter Three

Remembering Lincoln

Outside, we learn that some important events have taken place at the Lincoln Memorial. **Martin Luther King Jr.** spoke to a huge crowd from the steps in **1963**. He talked about his **dreams** for **fairness** for everyone.

Between two hundred thousand and three hundred thousand people gathered to hear King's speech.

"People still come here to remember President Lincoln's ideas," says Ranger May. "The Lincoln Memorial is a symbol of **fairness** and **togetherness**."

"What's a symbol?" asks Kim.

"A symbol is something that stands for something else," our guide answers. "Like a red light means stop."

We look out at **Washington, DC.** Our field trip is almost done.

"What do we tell Ranger May?" asks Mr. Williams.

"Thank you, Ranger May!" we shout.

The Lincoln Memorial is open every day, all day and all night. It is closed only on December 25.

On the bus, we talk about what President Lincoln and Martin Luther King Jr. dreamed for our country.

"What is **your dream**?" our teacher asks.

"I dream of flying to Mars!" says Martina.

"I'm dreaming of pizza," says Sebastian.

Mr. Williams says Sebastian must see the future. On the way home, we stop for pizza!

Make a Hand Impression

An artist made casts, or molds, of Abraham Lincoln's hands before he became president. Daniel Chester French studied these casts when he designed the statue for the Lincoln Memorial. You can make an impression of your own hands. Be sure to have an adult help you.

What You Need:

1 cup flour	baking sheet
1 cup salt	ruler
½ cup warm water	oven
bowl	cooling rack
mixing spoon	

1) Mix the flour, salt, and warm water in a bowl with a spoon. Use your hands to finish mixing the dough.

2) Form the dough into a ball. Then flatten it onto a baking sheet. The dough should be about ¾ inch (2 centimeters) thick.

3) Spread out your fingers. Push each of your hands, palms down, firmly into the dough.

4) Ask an adult to help put the baking sheet into the oven. Bake the dough at 100°F (38°C) or your oven's lowest setting for 3 hours.

5) Remove from the oven, set on a cooling rack, and let cool completely.

Look closely at the impressions of your hands. What details can you see?

GLOSSARY

civil war: a war between groups of people who live in the same country

column: a tall round pillar. Columns are often made of stone.

designed: made the plans for

founder: a person who starts something, such as a country or company

impression: a design made by pressing or stamping a surface

marble: a hard stone sometimes used for buildings and statues

memorial: a building or statue that helps us remember someone who died

slavery: keeping people as property and forcing them to work

symbol: something that stands for something else

united: together

Inside the memorial, words above the statue of Lincoln read, "In this temple, as in the hearts of the people for whom he saved the Union, the memory of Abraham Lincoln is enshrined forever."

TO LEARN MORE

BOOKS

Rappaport, Doreen. *Martin's Big Words: The Life of Martin Luther King Jr.*
New York: Hyperion Books, 2001.
Read quotes from King's writings and speeches in this picture book biography.

Winters, Kay. *Abe Lincoln: The Boy Who Loved Books.* New York: Simon & Schuster Books for Young Readers, 2003.
This picture book gives more information about Abraham Lincoln's life.

WEBSITES

Lincoln Memorial
http://www.nps.gov/featurecontent/ncr/linc/interactive/deploy/index.htm#/introduction
Take an interactive tour of the Lincoln Memorial at this National Park Service website.

Martin Luther King Jr.'s "I Have a Dream" Speech
http://www.youtube.com/watch?v=nFcbpGK9_aw
Watch part of King's famous speech at the Lincoln Memorial.

2009 Lincoln Cents
http://www.usmint.gov/kids/coinNews/cents/
See pictures of the four penny designs from 2009 that show different parts of Abraham Lincoln's life.

LERNER **e** SOURCE™

Expand learning beyond the printed book. Download free, complementary educational resources for this book from our website, www.lerneresource.com.

INDEX

Booth, John Wilkes, 16

Civil War, 10—11

columns, 8—9

King, Martin Luther, Jr., 18, 21

Lincoln, Abraham: death of, 16—17; as president, 4—5, 8—11, 12—15, 18—19, 21

slavery, 11, 15—16

speeches, 14—15, 19—20

states, 5, 9, 10—11, 14

statue, 7, 12—13